The Hidden I

Frederic Raphael

The Hidden I
A Myth Revised

Original drawings by
Sarah Raphael

Thames and Hudson

For George Steiner

Printed and bound in Great Britain
by Balding and Mansell.

The Hidden I

We begin on the shore of a sea with unclocked tides. The sand on which two young men are walking has never been impressed by a mechanical print. Their sandals are hand-cobbled; alike and unlike. The air they breathe is ripe with oxygen. Their blood is thicker than ours can ever be.

Lydia has wealth, but no money. It has language, but no literature. Its palaces have marble faces and golden tripes. Its tawny tutelary god is female. Her statues are protuberant: Artemis precedes art.

The clouds above the young men's almond heads are untainted by modern colours. When their sun sets, it lacks ironic undertones. Their daily sky is a blue we can only imagine. Why should Lydia want books when tomorrow will be as good as today and today is always as good as it is? (There are forests to the shore; rain hisses fertility.)

The young men's clothes contain no pockets. Without poetry or pennies, what should one keep in a pocket?

Are the young men dressed or are they naked on their drift of sand? They are not Greeks; are they trousered like the Persians (of whom they have scarcely heard)? They are naked *and* clothed, men.

They walk in a pasture of time in which choice and necessity have rubbed no fork. Each has his destiny. The grander the destiny, the smaller the choice. Choice is for slaves: "Work or die!" Free men are free of it.

There are weapons in Lydia, but none has the edge of gold. The king is master of its soft command. If gold bends, men bend with it. The king is lord of Lydia's treasury, but the queen determines who its lord shall be, and hers. Such is Lydia, a woman and a place, queen and country.

How should we tell, from unguarded appearances, which is the prince and which his friend? What timely symptoms denote royal priority, what ranking clues? Do you see that nose as an aristocrat's? Faces are texts; we read each other. But two young men, sleeved in elastic flesh, how shall we determine which is which?

The prince walks like a sleepwalker. He has no call to distinguish dream from reality. On *his* beach there are no stubbing rocks; on his friend's, there are. The friend takes steps to make things soft for the prince: he clears the way. Hence he is in front. The friend's caution is the prince's boldness; the leader follows, asserting precedence. He addresses the other's back as if it had alert eyes and tuned ears.

"My marriage. You've heard?"

"I've heard something."

There is attentive tact – yes and no – in the reply. The prince cannot see his friend's face as he addresses the horizon and, at the same time, throws pinched syllables, like lucky salt, over his shoulder.

"For instance?"

Is the friend's reply to swoop and shake a root free from the sand? There are many roots in the dunes. They wear instalments of bark and come to bossy heads. Children see animals in them, and men, and gods. They brush brisk sand from their beards and give them fearful names.

"It will change nothing. My marriage."

Is this a clown the friend has found, or a demon?

"Between us, I mean."

The friend befriends the whiskered wood and invites the prince, with turned head, to share his game. Is he curious to see the prince as he confesses his elevation? He does not indicate curiosity. He is acting. His name is Gyges. He does nothing, it seems, but attend to the prince. He hopes to entertain. The prince takes the root, as if he should be grateful. A stiff dragon, is it?

"We shall remain friends." Why does he find this clumsy to say? Because sincerity is not a style? "Exactly as we've always been."

Princes revel in peremptory reassurance.

The friend walks on. His sandals hyphenate the untidy sand. The prince hears yes and no in their lisping right and left. "I insist," he says.

Such insistence demands wit of the courtier. Silence is brevity prolonged. Gyges practises it.

"Forget what I'm going to be. Remember what I always was." The prince is giving dangerous instructions. He is teaching his friend to think for himself. Who will do as much for the prince? Whoever agrees to forget – as Gyges' bobbed head now does – also promises to remember. Oblivion is full of files; it triggers furtive muses.

"If I forget who you are" – does Gyges turn on this? – "I may talk to you only as if I were afraid." Timidity too can be brazen. Courage keeps the straighter face. "Is that what you want?"

"Do I follow you?" Candaules said (it was a common name in Lydia).

"The you I shall forget you are ..." His friend was frowning, as if he were the puzzled one. "Won't he be the boy I played with, when we were children? Yesterday! Or was it the day before? Can you expect me to forget the prince who is to marry Lydia? *That* you!"

"Oh but you must!"

"Must entails can't." Gyges aped the Greek who had taught them both (the way his bent lips covered his toothless gums when he smiled). "Am I being more candid than I should?"

There was a hand on his shoulder. "Candour always hides something." Candaules was proving that he too had had lessons in paradox. "The truth is an agreed lie."

"White," Gyges quoted, "is the name of all the colours."

The boyish past was bracketed between them, dew pearled between windy leaves.

As a remembered shower hazed the sun, before muttering in the dust, it warped into prismatic hoops. The Greek slave, his wrists unmanacled by brains, drew arch conclusions with both hands. The young men were his memorial, his marbles.

"When I am king," Candaules said, closing the bracket, "you will be the one person in the kingdom to whom I shall always be able to talk. And from whom I shall always expect the truth."

"And I hoped," his friend dared to say, "that we might stay friends!"

Fear flatters. The prince wanted to touch it. It made him fond. The two understood something which was not in the present, and made a present of it for each other. They shared a future which would exclude one or the other. Their humour came of what they realised and did not. They could have kissed.

This is the Lydian light in which a handsome prince and his more handsome friend are walking, in the hot evening of their youth, along the cuff of a rich kingdom which one of them is due to rule. If the prince looks on his friend as his equal, that is the measure of their inequality.

"Look at that glorious sun!" One says this as it sets. Who looks at it in its glory?

The prince assumes himself as handsome as the other. Gyges is a breathing mirror in which Candaules believes that he can see himself. Its flaw is its virtue: where Gyges bows, the prince looks straight.

This coast has no piers. Nothing in the dream escapes significance; in reality nothing escapes accountancy. What we do not have is part of us.

Why should the prince be less handsome? This ruddying evening he has more than the advantages of blood and lineage; there is also the gloss of election. Yet he looks to his comely companion for reassurance. He must confirm that he really and truly is what no one – himself apart – doubts him to be. Can he then be it?

"Box on," the Greek would say.

Strutting in the luxury of liberty, the young men reach a slump of sand where pumice floats, unrooted evidence of ancient catastrophe. There are no facilities for conflict here, but the prince frowns the whorled space into a gymnasium.

"Can you still jump?"

"Jump?" There is an unvoiced void – blank, blank, blank – just three letters long, after the prince's friend has spoken. It leaves room for S,I,R. Gyges remembers what he has been commissioned to forget. He plays equality; he breathes subversion. The climate grows instant courtiers.

"Jump. As we did after lessons with the Greek. Make a mark, Gyges, in the sand and we'll run and jump and see who wins. You can't have forgotten."

"How to jump? Hardly."

"Promise you'll do your best. If you don't, where's the pleasure in beating you?"

All duels are sweet in their preliminaries. Before the threshold, every move is dandy: selection of the site, choice of weapons, well-sprung carriages. Complicity begins to marry the contestants. Their seconds take on the duties of antagonism whose principals are spared. They alone are exempt from taking sides, who first divided them. The assignation exalts those who must present it with their blood. Brief immortals, they cannot imagine dying save at the crucial junction, up ahead, where lifelines cross. All coming wars bless warriors with provisional immunity; how can they catch today's cold who march to tomorrow's drum? Games are battles' buttoned doubles; if corked foils carry no killing point, their timed hostilities conscript savagery's cousin. Courteous courage is prompt to the changing room. Marriage buttons and unbuttons its contestants. In love and war, and in their playful parodies, rites lend logic to the accidental: we double gods in them. That rendezvous with death once entered, like some brave party, in his diary, the duellist transcends the coarse uncertainty of any mortal month: the red-lettered world turns on him as he on his dearest foe. No longer labile wax, wicked candle, he is all fused flame. The duel steepens life towards its climax, the bang. Murder and pleasure, under licence, share amenities.

"Which hand is it in?"

"Sorry?"

"Which hand is it in? Is something wrong?"

Gyges' hesitation is for both their pleasures. They dwell on the prospect of elective enmity, relish sentiments they cannot express. A wordless bubble rallies between them. They observe its irised fragility, primed with the sun's decline. Who is thinking of blood? Prelude or postlude, which is this? Language has no currency for such exchanges.

We have not come to money yet; it is not time. The mouth (remember) was the first pocket, though for the present only words are kept there; and silences. Desire comes, like a butler, uncalled for, and cannot supply what they want. There is purity in their embarrassment, and wicked winks.

"Suppose," Gyges said, "you don't win."

"Remember who you are, my friend!" The prince's smoothness rehearses an official beard. See him handsome and strong. Gyges does. His only ugliness lies in the fear of being ugly. (The solipsist is never alone, the Greek would say.) If he has a weakness – the prince, the prince! – it is for proofs of strength. (Herakles was only half a god.)

The man whose ambition has been realised always finds his enemy in time. His future is cloaked like an assassin. "Remember who you are!"

The mirrors of Lydia are *terracotta*. They are frying pans which cannot endure the fire. Once cooked, they are done. Filled with water, they furnish soft mirrors. Women pan for beauty in them as prospectors for gold. When they find it, they worry: where is beauty to be safely kept? It is a perishable treasure, once the calendar is known.

These two young men, how did they meet? At school? Do men ever meet anywhere else? Gyges was presented to the prince like a puppy too young to guess what kind of pet he was meant to be. It all seemed natural to him, and to the other. He would be second, it was planned, in a class of two, instructed by the Greek. He would run and jump with Candaules between lessons. Only the eyes of rounded supernumeraries knew how purposeful play could be. How can the young man say how good he has been, so far, in what he assumes an artless role?

Ambition is a kitten surprised by a mirror; it can never recognise itself. Puzzled, it paws and tilts its head at the alien vision, itself, scentless and unattainable. How can something be and not be? I is another! What grammar is staunch against appetite?

Every idol ever overthrown was first polished and revered by those who came to smash it. Who is more reliable, more obsessive in his deference, than the traitor? It is always safe to leave him with the keys. Does anyone look straighter than the spy? He is the unblinking knave who promises no other eye.

Is Gyges a spy? Loyally, he awaits his vocation.

The beauty of games, however simple their original pre-
miss, is that they must – if they are to enter the playful
repertoire – secrete moves and subtleties beyond the capac-
ity of their inventors to have foreseen. The ancient game is
a scabbard sleeving the modern. Everything that is the
same is also different. Cheating depends on playing the
game; adultery on marriage! Treason is a tribute to
monarchy.

Is the long jump a game? Can one cheat at it?

Gyges takes the dragon root and scores a cleft in the
labile sand.

"Who jumps first?" Gyges wants things straight,
doesn't he?

"You decide."

"The gods can decide." He shows agility in palming
pumice. "Which hand's it in?"

The prince frowns at the two fists. Faced with choice,
indifference dons suspicion like a borrowed hat. "That
one?" The hint of a question makes Gyges responsible.
"That one!"

His friend shows Candaules air. He lets it go like a fin-
ger-caged butterfly. "You lose. You can jump first."

Naked, Candaules has not thrown his hat aside. "We
should have defined what it meant to guess wrong, before
you decided I'd lost."

"Whatever the terms, you didn't *win*, did you? Can it matter who jumps first? We each jump; we each do our best. Can my best be better, or worse, because you jumped before me? Would you do better if you knew how well I was going to do?"

"*Had* done," says the prince. "And that's enough of that."

"Time is relative," says Gyges, ahead of the game.

"And what is not?"

"True!" Doubt rides pillion on endorsement; sceptics embrace certainty from behind. "Why jump at all? What proof or pleasure will come of it? Let's drop the whole thing."

Candaules will not be underestimated. "We said we would; we shall."

"Look," says his playmate, "start again, if you want. Define the rules and then we'll keep them. Which hand now?"

"If I lose again," the prince pouts, "I shall repeat myself. If I win, I shall remember only that I lost before. And why, after all, should I be the one put to the guess? You know and I guess; is that equality?"

"Your chances of winning are the same as mine."

"Are they, my friend, when you already know what I must guess? The chances may be the same; the pleasures are not. As if it mattered!" The prince is noble. "I'll jump first."

He paces back from the paling mark in the sand. He smiles at Gyges, as enemies will.

In this contest there are no second chances. Nor is there common experience. One man is idle as the other performs; when one is still fresh, the other will be done. They do this together, separately. There may be brothers; there are no twins.

The prince takes steadying breaths. He consults the unchemical sky. He rehearses his run in energetic postponement. Gyges' eyes have business elsewhere; he winks at the wind. The prince hangs naked, soft-sceptred. Gyges takes care not to look, for fear of seeming interested. Soon he must show himself.

The prince, done with pacing, stands at his own petty score, ready. He will have Gyges look at him. Gyges, commanded, looks. The prince fills and empties his lungs and flings himself towards the mark. Gyges attends. Hurdling the air, the prince makes his strident leap.

Heels; knees; palm; shoulder; knee; feet. He looks back. Gyges' caption: Orpheus misses Eurydice.

"Very good. Indeed."

"Can you beat it? Beat it if you can."

"Why wouldn't I?"

Can questions lie?

Gyges too makes his preparations, his postponing play. He mimes his run. Limbering fingers contrive a lyre of the unstrung air. How shall he do this so that good consequences may flow? What performance will damage the future, what enhance it? In any crucial act there is no reliable rehearsal. At critical moments, everyone is virgin.

Gyges is kitted with all the symptoms of fear. The best he hopes for is not to disgrace himself. A good second will be good enough for him, would you not say so? The prince becomes his coach. "Courage, my friend!" Gyges' strength is his duplicity. He is and he is not himself, whoever that may be. He does not know what he wants; only that he wants it. His lungs are bricked with air. He is about to win or lose, but what is he about?

The prince lolls at the mark. Moustached with sweat (as if he were still exerting himself), his body is gored by the setting sun. No longer in the competition, he becomes an official. Going first has aged him.

Does Gyges know that he can beat the prince? Or does he fear that he may? Then again, does he fear that, doing his best, he will fall behind the raked bruise where the prince came down? Can he face being the inferior which, on consideration, he might choose to be? (To lose is not always to be beaten.) How wise would it be to outjump the man who will be Lydia?

"Are you ever going to jump?"

Gyges turns at the limit of his run. Exhilaration unsleeves him from fear. Naked, he puts on manhood. The prince is beached on one elbow. Gyges takes loosening strides, quickens his pace, reaches the shadowed cleft and takes to the empty ladder of the sky. One step, two, he pedals the void.

Below him is the prince's spent place in the pit. Gyges must, it seems, either overfly it or not. In his long moment of wingless flight, Gyges solves himself (the equation should always bear his name); he perceives an alternative to victory or defeat. No two without a three! Grammar too has its physics.

With ingenious accuracy, Gyges lands precisely in the footprints of the prince. He collapses into the other like a noonday shade: heels, knees, palm, shoulder.

Gyges is rich in carbon; copying is the condition of survival, and advancement. Admire the inventive resource (fear duplicitous with hope) with which he looks back at the place where his victorious landing might be flared, or the blemish of defeat declared. There is no hint of either thing.

"Dead heat! Gyges, you're the invisible man! No sign of you anywhere!" The prince thinks he reports a fact, not a decision. Nature is bent; he sees it straight. He remains a man of his time; Gyges reads a different clock.

"You didn't do that on purpose, did you?"

"Do you think anyone could?"

The sun makes unwarming coals of the sea.

Sweat braids their brows in salt fraternity. Comradeship and cunning sport common colours. Gyges is twin: the good brother and the bad. He offers no return (not having won, why should he?). The prince has no notion that his friend may be a jump ahead of him. Candaules has granted equality (confirming his grace); how should he suspect that his friend has dared to contrive it? Fear outjumped, everything is easy now for Gyges. How modestly he blows out his cheeks in affable relief! "I didn't think I was going to make it."

The play begins. To Memory, a daughter.

The naked prince touches his naked friend. How could they possibly be closer, when they are indistinguishable? The prince is nice enough – if innocence is nice – not to realise that three of them are coupled there.

"Now what? Do we try again?"

"A tie is victory enough for me, sir. Parity is a promotion in my case. I trust it no disappointment to you."

"It's all the same to me." Do we hear petulance in the prince's off-duty tone? When things are all the same it always makes a difference. Has the prince begun to realise – will he ever realise? – that no courtier can be sincere?

Sincerity is not a method in art. Art begins with patrons, not with artists: we hunt, you stay in the cave.

The pair of them walk back towards the city. The Greek taught them the dual case because it was in the grammar. It announced a couple, and their actions. " 'We two,' " he informed them, "has a separate form from 'you two', but" – here the lips flexed inwards – "but they are identical!"

The boys laughed. Two and two were one.

"What do you say to a woman?"

In the precinct of the temple, women waited for men. Some of the women were mantled; some showed themselves. Surrender and defiance had the same legs. The women's show deterred those who shunned the ugly and those who flinched from the judgment of the beautiful. Ugliness and beauty were sisters then, were they?

Men suspected that some women returned, veiled, for voluntary pleasure. Suspicion and optimism rode tandem in the male mind. They watched, bold and embarrassed, by the women's pillared precinct.

A little man, tall dwarf, with a crooked back and a thick stick, went to a serene woman who wore gilt sandals. He touched her like a beast with the knob of his stick. Did the prince, at that moment, want her as Gyges did?

The woman turned back the droop of her mantle. She gazed at the man with loud black eyes. Her submission was an order.

He followed her to a place by the low wall. His eyes invited the friends. He touched the nape of the woman's neck, an expert with a cub. Paws on the wall, the temporary sphinx crouched. He lifted the hem of her woollen robe and comforted her waist. White coloured the ready purse. The little man stalled his stick in a snake-hole.

The beauty was his because he had chosen her. He rode with his feet on the ground. When he grinned at them he did not conceal his gums. He had his teeth. The woman looked at them too, but they did not look back.

The prince cleared his throat as they filed the sphinx and her rider in their museum: new acquisition. He spoke of his plans. He had been thinking. Lydia needed new buildings: how else should ambassadors report her well in Egypt? The preliminaries – to be frank – might be a bore (or a challenge), but all his apprehensions (you know how it is with weddings) were fused in the glorious prospect of power.

Gyges the good listener made a giant of the working dwarf. His chest was hard with air, as though he had yet to jump. The dwarf's white strength, when it showed, could have been his.

"Are we going to find someone," he said, "or not?"

"Seen anyone you could want?"

"Not here," Gyges said.

"Nor I."

The two men are friends again. It is pleasant to lie together.

The prince leads. On the way to the girl Gyges wears informality like a boxer's gown. Even with the girl there will be occasion for tact. He sweats before the next round. (Shadows can punch.) Should a diplomat come first or second? Can another dead heat be procured, another breathless coincidence? Is wisdom wise? The prince thinks the contest over; for Gyges, it has no bell.

The city shows scant light. Smoke furs the evening, but no windows advertise. The place is a burrow, battened below ground. Ladders plumb its floors. The friends go down.

Imagine a woman's eyes on them! Would that change anything, or everything? An addition always changes things; it takes something away (the Greek told them). Can two men ever be the same when a woman is watching?

Lydia is in her palace, behind canted walls. Her towers alone show above the ground. Who guesses from those straw-shagged battlements that there is gold within? Can a certainty be guessed? Lydia is gold; she sees herself in it: her mirrors need no watering. The palace boasts what it hides. She is the queen and, wherever Lydia is, she is. Unless the men would be exiles, they are in her sight. They have no choice.

The prince laughs – since he is unamused – when he tells his friend that he has never seen the queen to whom he is promised. In the skyless streets, revetted with bamboo, heat makes a body of the place. As they go down, escaping light flukes them and leaves them snuffed in shadows again. Anonymity is a toy the prince appreciates. Soon he will be denied its playful amenities. Purple office will make obscurity a privilege. He envies Gyges, who will have less then he.

Every young man before his marriage sees it as a kind of death. He goes into it as soldiers go into battle. What else can he do, the boy, the man?

The friends commission a girl. She oils her hands from a jar snubbed in the corner of her pit. She rinses them till they shine. Her nails are black. One on each hand is sanded flush with the glistening cap of flesh she makes a probable promise.

They look at each other over the stopped saddle of the girl. Twenty fingers ply her. In the toil of pleasure, they are on opposite sides, together. The Median girl has metered hopes. Her eyes solicit gratitude and prompt impatience. She would belong to the one she denies. Someone always has to wait.

The queen, a woman never seen in public, is being dressed for her wedding. There is a recipe: the clothes, the foliage. The air is sauced with frankincense. Sardis, her capital, steams like a midden; in the palace, nasal luxuries are needed.

Priests put on copious importance. The day is their slave. A commissioned seer surveys pelts and feathers. His victims are his favourites. He must find happy livers.

The prince has all the attentions accorded the condemned: breakfast, privacy before the crowd. He is the fool who must be treated with solemnity. That is the joke. Every victim – high or low – has heard the story, witnessed the play. Rules conjure prospects of exception. The annual criminal, given victuals and pristine raiment (he appreciates the archaic touch), plays the eager peacock. He bestrides his narrow principality for an eternal year before the rent is due. Then he is driven to the limit, dunned with more or less friendly stones, slashed low with impersonal accuracy; made it, not him. The carnivore cliff, the cuspid rocks, the swallowing sea, he is their meat. They swear, who crowned and cursed him, that he chose freely to be the red bolt in their machine. And did he not? Did he not know his fate? He knew, but he could not believe. All men are mortal; the future is their terrible tense, yet they conjugate hope in it.

The couple cannot now escape. They know nothing of each other save their common destination. The queen's decision has decided her. Duty? Love? Translations both!

Blindfold teams work the millstones. The circle is an endless line. The dry juice is squeezed and dust is bred. Bakers play Columbine, costumed in flour. In the pens by the virgin's temple, white victims jostle with the flawed stock whose faults reprieve them.

Must the queen be in the same case as her chosen? She is being dressed perhaps, but she is scarcely a victim; her bridal stuff is not all white. If Lydia creates the king, by selecting him, how shall her condition pair with his? She is sovereign here. Did she take advice from wise counsellors? What man ever wore wisdom in his breeches? They are all fools there. Dress the prince as custom or fancy stipulates: stiffen his sceptre/stud his crown/pad his cods. She knows him before he knows her. Lydia is queen.

Has there been a funeral? Has another king gone up in smoke? Must our couple mount steps scraped from ash? Is a queen dead and supplanted, a new royal avenue bannered for traffic? Every story is defective; it dances with an unseen partner. There is a wedding; society salutes what flatters it. The citizens observe robes, sacerdotal obligation, knives. Priests do their learned business. When was a choir innocent and applauded? They have been here before, even the trebles.

An early market primes the day. Stalled colours sweeten in the usual sun. Wheels with wooden pins and hoofed engines, goddess-eyed, roll in dew-dottled dust. The palace gates open like an articulated flower. Smiling guards?

The priests, from good families, put on flamboyant anonymity. Their masks surge with the god. The nodding victim, offered terms, agrees to die. Slashed red, the perfect bull has shorter legs, prays (the knees give it away) and invests beef in the royal pair. The pit (and pity?) for him who stains the day.

Pieces move in the prescribed opening. No feelings are expressed; none need be felt. Ritual cannot be patched with sentiment. There is no talk of better or worse. We hear no account of how long anyone has known the bride, or the prince's father. The thing done is the done thing; nothing else need be imported. Rice is not required.

Music scores the afternoon and makes the sunset voluntary. The sky is sieved with lucky stars. Lady moon pulls sea to sand. Candaules, king, honours the tidal calendar: he is drawn to the palace in a woolly chariot. Moon-veiled modesty rides beside him: Lydia.

The night is coarse with relief. What was feared in the light is mocked on the secret decks of the city. The palace gates heal.

Gyges is without his friend. The prince is ticketed with a victim's brand. King and queen are stiff with the halter of words; everything has now been said and they feel the weight they no longer carry. They have strained in ritual obedience. A slip would mean beginning all over again. Under those circumstances, who would not be pious?

"Are you as hungry as I am?"

The priests have steak for dinner. The gods must sup on smoke. (Comedy begins with their deception; tragedy gives them the last laugh.)

Gyges tramps the night streets amid the rinds of celebration. Today is in shreds at his feet. The gutter is soppy with wine and water. Rejoicing stales into snores; toasts yellow. Liberated and desolate, Gyges is a sentry without a beat. He walks the depressed capital bare of his favourite fetters. A sigh of relief remains a sigh. If his friend still has his number, he will not call for a while. Enjoy yourself, Gyges, why can't you?

Does Gyges envy Candaules? Or the queen her king?

How many feelings are distinguishable here? How many sides to a triangle? How few?

Stiff clothes have made a secret of the queen. No tall dwarf has steeped himself in her. Imagination's larder is unstocked. How shall Gyges envy his friend, the king, who has been digested into the royal house? The two-mouthed whore may have married them; the queen is their divorce.

In the bracket of his reign, a sovereign's early years – the attendant time before accession – count for nothing. He is dated only from the moment of enthronement; his minority, however long, excites no arithmetic. Thus do kings live less long than other men. They are pinched in tighter brackets, however sumptuous.

Unsponsored normality kits the streets. The royal road is lumbered with obvious traffic. Exchange is the muscle of the state; it grows strong on it. The road up and the road down is a double donkey working Sardis-Ephesus.

Gyges enjoys virile activities. Spared the demanding privilege of royal intimacy, he thinks of what he need not, in voiceless luxury. Reprieve and release are two hands of the same wide gesture. Which is the honour? Which the threat?

Late light stabbed through wounds in the camel ceiling as Gyges was splashing salt from his leathered face, after setting javelins through a straw heart or two. Three men strode their boots into the domed baths.

"Come with us, please."

Arrest and preferment are the left and right which lead us to powerful presences. Gyges was escorted to the gate in

a roasted flank of the palace. If he smiled at those who looked and did not look at him on the way, was it resignation or engagement? The king wanted something of him. Might it be his life?

Within the metalled cedar, he smells the coming yellow. He follows a eunuch into a golden world. He has heard of the wealth within the dung-bricked walls; now he sees it. It gilds him.

Candaules is robed in white. He wears unscuffed sandals. They have never known the merchants' ruts or the gutters' slurry. The king's steps are unsoiled.

The king's face is jaundiced. Muscles have sweetened to butter. Gyges is no longer his mirror.

"Sit down, my friend. We're alone." It sounds like a lie (why say it otherwise?), although there is no one else in the room. Gyges takes inventory. What are those things, mummied in sacking, against the valuable wall?

"Come, come, look at me. You haven't changed." Implying: "Have I?" So that, "Have I?", when first voiced, sounds like impatient repetition.

"Your majesty looks very well. Stronger. More . . ."

"Well?"

"*More*!" Evasiveness looks the king full in the eye. Trust deceit.

"I can rely on you to be clever. Can I rely on you to be anything else? Because tell me the truth. I've missed you, but I've also missed *it*. Be my oracle. More what?"

"Yourself, sir. I have never known you more!"

"I eat well; I exercise a little. You mean I'm fat."

"You were always a big man. Now you are . . . officially big. It's part of you, greater than the whole you were!"

"The truth is always an evasion with you, my friend. Why not be straight?"

"We live in nature, sire. Geometry is not my subject, nor can I be its."

"Why have I missed you so much?"

"Because I have not been here. Had I been here ..."

"Yet here you are! Reconciling caution and boldness like a true courtier. You are counterfeit only in this: you amuse me. They do not. Only don't tell them so."

"His majesty flatters me."

"His majesty needs you, Gyges."

"And what more flattering than that! I am at your majesty's service. That is all I am. Or should be, I might add."

"You play at distance, but you remember how close we were? Interchangeable! What was her name?"

"She had a name? I took her for a number."

"And our dead heat. Don't tell me you've forgotten that!"

"In subjects, majesty, silence *is* memory."

"They are statues, Gyges."

"What's that, sire?"

"They are lagged gods. The things you are not looking at so keenly. Why are you here, Gyges?"

"They came for me, sire. I was outnumbered. Here I am."

"I knew I had missed you; I had forgotten why. You make me laugh. Sometimes. Shall I tell you something? Why not, now? You may not believe this, but I always felt that I had only *just* managed to run as fast as you, jump as long, throw the javelin as far. I always felt that I came

second in our equality, the cheaper twin. Absurd, you're right, in the light of today, but there it was."

Gyges had no line; he supplied a pause.

"You're still wondering why I sent for you. To tell you something I always feared you might be relieved to hear: I no longer need you. I'm free; so are you."

"Your majesty is very . . . generous."

"What did you reject, Gyges? As an adjective? I like hidden things."

"Honest." Who could guess that it was the choosing of what he would *not* say which had delayed him? On his way to the door, backing, he smiled, as if he would have spoken, had a third person (who was not there) not been present. Him or her? The king said he liked hidden things.

"Did I say you were to go?"

"I assumed . . ."

"Are you happy, Gyges?"

"As the king is happy, so must his subjects be."

"You cannot be happier than I am."

"Our grammar forbids it; to deny it is treason. Our hearts rejoice in its assertion."

"Yes, yes, yes. Don't you want to know why? Not because you are no longer my friend, but because I no longer need you to be. I have not changed towards you, Gyges, but I have changed. You are my *better* friend, but you are no longer my best. Are you not curious for an explanation?"

"I am happy for your majesty. How should I need an explanation for my humble duty?"

"Can any man be happy for another? Today I could jump clear over the horizon. Do you believe me?"

"The king commands belief."

"Tell me why. Why?"

"Kingship fits you like a woollen cap."

"Woollen caps fit everybody. You can do better than that. Tell me the reason."

"When did happiness ever room with reason?"

"Because Lydia is rich in gold and chariots? Because the Persians fawn? Their ambassador! Because ships ply into Ephesus buoyant with successful sails? I am happy for one reason, Gyges."

"Sire?"

"You have not jumped one inch! Lydia is beautiful."

"She is indeed the envy of other states."

"The queen, you clown!"

"Who doubts it, sire?"

"I married in fear; I reign in joy. The queen."

The throne-room sizzles as Gyges rehearses embarrassment. He looks down. He looks up.

"What's that noise?"

"A bee, majesty, scouting pollen in the golden petals of your ceiling."

The highflown buzzing covers the shiver of emotion in Gyges. He cannot say what he feels, but he feels that he feels it. He stands beside himself, straight man and comic: the player.

"She is more beautiful than words can even hint."

"I can well believe it."

"No, you cannot, because she surpasses belief. Belief

will always jump short of the truth. Inaccuracy is the laziest of flatteries. You are silent."

Gyges is. Being right does not please the king.

"You think me a babbler."

"Never."

"You thought before you spoke. You do, and with cause. I babble because what I know is beyond expression. We need a poet here."

"Offer prizes."

"If only you could see for yourself how beautiful she is. You would be my poet. You have no idea . . ."

"I was at the wedding, sire."

"Where you saw only the space she filled. Nothing – and no more – is what you saw, dressed in nuptial robes. You saw the breathing of her veil, never her lips. If you could only see what I've seen, and see, every night."

Gyges said, "These statues . . ."

"If only you could."

"May your majesty's happiness endure forever."

"You are the only person in the world I can talk to."

Gyges scores a mark.

"I was obliged," the husky king goes on, "to marry a woman who, had I known what she was like, I should have fought the whole world to possess."

The old grammarian was grinning toothlessly in Gyges.

"Would I have allowed even my best friend to come between me and her? Treachery and honour would have carried the same accent for her sake! Remember our Greek? The dual and the duel, one! I was forced – you know that – to accept a prize worth a lifetime of wounds and labours to acquire. Today I would wrestle Herakles for her. I am the happiest man in the world. Do I repeat myself? I have only one grief."

"One is enough. When there is a pair they can multiply. May your majesty's grief remain uncoupled."

"That my only friend can never know how fortunate I am."

"He can hear. If he is present. And rejoice, when he is not. Deprivation is a bonus here."

"Are you in a hurry to be gone? The only man to whom I can speak with candour. In all the colours! Don't lower me, Gyges, by lowering yourself. Be up to it, man. We've been in a dead heat, you and I."

"You are far ahead of me now, and warrant your priority."

"Don't be diplomatic. Don't, please, be tactful; I shall be more touched if you are not."

"I shall never touch your majesty."

"Damn your elegance, man. We shared holes, you and the boy I was. Don't imagine Lydia has anything in common with that mercenary drab."

"Such a thought is inconceivable."

"I hear its bawdy cackle, like a slave girl's child. All thoughts can be conceived. Who can swat the last fly? I want you to see her for yourself."

"The embassy from Egypt must be received. There will, I presume, be a banquet."

"She dresses for banquets. I want you to see her."

"I beg your majesty excuse me."

"For my sake. Would you deny your king? Be careful!"

"For his sake, I might. For his sake, I might be very careful."

"You deny me perfect happiness."

"When it is yours? Never."

"It cannot be mine unless my friend agrees with me."

"I agree."

"Words are worthless without knowledge. Beauty must be seen. I insist. Think what it will mean, when we look at each other, our silence when we see each other; you will be one with me. You have no choice, Gyges."

"Except to go."

"Nothing will change."

"Then let us change nothing."

"There is a place I can conceal myself . . . I'll show you. Oh yes, I've already done it. I admit it: I tried to be you. To enjoy the virgin pleasure of seeing Lydia when she takes herself to be alone. She undresses as if she were a lover, without knowing what she does, the beauty. What do you say?"

Stubbed in the slave girl's oiled place, Gyges looked at his friend. Gyges looked at the king now.

"I will show you."

"My lord, I do not deserve this. I do not deserve it."

"She will never know. No one will ever know. You and I and no one else."

Men like to think that women do not know what they are doing, or what they have done to them. How else shall knowledge remain a man's club? The committee is glad to announce ladies' nights, of course. The last one was a particular success. The wife, the ladies, the girls, how much they mean to us!

"You will never," the king says, as they go through cedar doors, "never see a more beautiful sight."

"Permit me ..." They have reached a corner; Gyges would prefer a wall.

"I will permit you anything, Gyges, once you have done as we ask. I must have my happiness fully understood by someone, or how shall we be happy? The Greek would be amused, would he not, to hear me use the dual so selfishly? Wait till you see her."

"Permit me to wait forever, sire."

"Happiness must be shared or it is dream."

"Your majesty shares it with Lydia. The rest of us live in your light: the sun, the moon."

"Without sight, how can you be enlightened? A woman's beauty cannot be shared with her; she cannot see it as we do. Come, man."

"Your majesty invites me to treason."

"Disobey the king, what else are you committing?"

"The queen is Lydia."

"Did I send for a lawyer? Do you put yourself on a par with me? Are we two pawns in her shadow? I am king in the queen. You are good at tight spots; turn in this one. I've got you, my friend. A pawn in check!"

Can the guard behind the lion door say which of them is laughing? When did laughter carry a certain signature? Do they both laugh? Neither is amused. That is the joke.

"Obey me, Gyges, or die!" Is that a joke? "I'm serious." His laugh certifies it. "If you ever loved me, do as I ask. Would you sooner go and live in dismal Athens? Do you fancy life with the cityless Spartans? Physical jerks with the girls, to the sound of flutes! Eat *porridge*? Or will you consent to dine with your king, in return for a service which will not hurt you and cannot conceivably hurt her?

Please. Please me, and I will make you the most powerful man in the kingdom. Have you no ambition, man?"

"At the moment, sire, porridge smells like the choicest cut. The ambition you suggest reeks of the unspeakable. I leave power to the powerful."

"A bequest not in your gift, Gyges. I meant the most powerful after me."

"Am I relieved? I am trapped; there is no relief in that."

"Where's the harm in it? Take my secret place just once; it will be as if it never happened."

"It will be," says Gyges, "as if it always happened."

"Refuse and it's your head. I mean it."

Gyges nods, the victim at the altar when the priests produce the fatal titbit.

The king and his cowed friend smile together unguardedly, as if naked and bound for the same act. Their reflections flex and flow together on the luscious walls as they reach the private apartments. Their even pace on the floor swells and swirls on the golden surface of the irregular walls. They fatten and lose weight in each other's eyes.

This is where the queen's robes are racked like empty promises. Gyges is her stand-in, condemned to privilege. Her dresses whisper at the intruder.

"When Lydia has disrobed, she will go into our bedroom, to wait for me. Once she leaves the undressing room, you are free to go, my friend."

"And if I am seen?"

"Prove your wit."

"Bodyguards have scant sense of humour."

"Take this ring. Whoever wears the king's ring need

never explain himself. Show it and you are as good as invisible."

"Goodbye, sire. You will never see me again."

"Again *and* again. You'll see."

The king closes the dowelled door of the secret place and breathes new flavours. He returns along the corridor where, moments earlier, the images of himself and his friend were placarded, heads and tails. He is alone with indelible company: the thought of Gyges and the thought of Lydia.

Gyges is alone in the secret camera, the hanging space, the pending file.

The king is rejuvenated by time's reverse: through Gyges he will enjoy Lydia again for the first time. The unique will have a double: the cheat.

Gyges' body hangs about him as the queen's dresses hang over shaped emptiness. He too is waiting to be put upon the queen. He will be the invisible net that catches every part of her. Can he be as vacant as fable would make him? The innocent wax carries its blank like a scar. Gyges' character is stunned, not dead. Here is a nobleman primed to nail a straw target or its fleshed surrogate from a galloping chariot. He can judge closing distances and aim off to compensate. How shall he now not quicken like a warrior, being the same, as he sees destiny in a swirl of coming dust?

Gyges wears the king's ring; he is in the king's hole. Out of dread, by necessity, springs ambition, jockeyed by opportunity.

The king, in courteous mimicry of what everyone takes him to be, lends the royal ear to a canting secretary, as if such entertainment were a pleasure. Was anyone ever more gracious to an accountant than Candaules to his?

Imagine a thoughtless man and there is no one there, the brute. Gyges has his head and means to keep it. He can close his eyes, but the mind skips their fence; it is faster than light. Will she be beautiful? Or will he be ashamed of a king who sees a goddess in a stale? Which option is more comfortable? Can this woman – she is coming now – possibly be what the king believes her to be? Is Gyges?

"Can I do anything else for you, sire?"

"Nothing. At once."

"Goodnight, sire."

Taking herself to be alone, the queen lets down her hair. The fuse of curiosity is lit in Gyges. All Lydia is revealed to him. He sees. Imagine. Gyges has; and is trumped.

The questing bee is heard to buzz. The queen – about to cover herself – gasps gentle alarm. The humble insect denies her modesty. Naked and distressed – oh the gleam of the hair! – she turns detective for fear of the sting. She tilts her head, that head, and shows her throat. She leans, flat-footed (thus the hips), to catch the intruder's tune. She touches herself with the heel of her hand behind and below her busy ear. She looks for the bee, and for Gyges, all eyes.

The bee buzzes and is quenched. Gyges is stung by his decision. The bee between thumb and forefinger, pinched present, is a painful flower. The queen listens, puzzled, to the silence: has she heard it before? Gyges is unlipped, but he has his teeth. Hurt, pride, fear mark his wax.

The queen is pleased, and a woman. Her flesh is easy. She shivers in delivery. Alone and in company, she smiles, the beauty. She is not a goddess; she does not blind. Gyges can see what the king has had.

The vision magics Gyges to water. The queen, fears all spent, turns away and snags on the glint of him. He flashes like a swinish mirror and she catches a low sight of herself, the beaded badge. She feels the man's eyes on her heat and is nettled with happiness, for the last time: she thinks him the king, her majesty.

"I know you're there, aren't you? You might as well come out. I know exactly where you are." Her voice was their baby; it crawled cooing towards him. "Come out, my love, my darling. I belong to you, and yet you spy! Why be a boy when I know you a man? Come out. Do you imagine I can't tell when you're looking at me? Why hide?"

The dowel mills dust. Gyges is her man.

"Who are you?" The queen's voice grows up.

"Your majesty's most unfortunate subject."

"Why?"

"Because I am utterly without excuse." He is her beastly toy; he would have her play with him. "Call the guard, majesty; have him kill me right away."

"That might be too soon."

"As you wish." Abject, he has no shame as he has no hope. "But cover yourself." Servile, he insists. "I beg you."

"You have an excuse. You must."

"None."

"Liar."

"I swear."

"Perjury."

"True. I deserve to die."

"It is your excuse you want destroyed, never yourself. You're hiding something. What's that?"

His swollen thumb and white forefinger let the striped flatness button the flags. "I feared you were afraid."

"*Why* ...?"

"Isn't it obvious?"

"... has he done this to me when I loved him?" A terrible clock is in motion. She has put the king in the past. "You, presumably, are his coward."

"Your majesty is a brave woman." Gyges' eyes are gorgeous with the queen. "But I beg you, cover yourself!"

Her body swims in stillness, very life, the thing. She punishes him with the sight of it. "You have seen me once," she says, "you have seen me forever. I am Lydia. And what are you? Worse, what is he?"

"He? Who?"

"Don't play the donkey."

"I acted alone, your majesty, like a worm. Please believe me. I deserve to die."

"And shall, my hypocrite! You're an actor, but you're not alone in this. Show me your hand. The other one, you clown!"

"I am also a thief."

"How did you come by this? When? Where?"

"I took it without his knowing."

"You're his lover?"

"I was his friend."

"You mean to die slowly. Or can it be that you – who heap treason on treason like a dishy waiter – have a stock of lives? Are you perhaps some shifty god, smirking at hermetic powers? Shall I play mother *and* the fool?"

"Neither at my hands."

"Do you understudy oracles or inspire them with your snake's denials? He gave it to you, did he not?"

"Put something on, your majesty."

"The dog gives orders? What is it to me that you see me?"

"Nothing, I trust."

"And I trust nothing. Is that lordship or slavery? Remove your clothes."

"I beg you spare me."

"Embarrassment? What can your excitement mean to me? I have seen curs go pink beneath their skulking bellies when I pass and dust their heat in shame. Oh their silly eyes! I want to see you as you saw me. *See* me! Do as I say, you woman."

The sorry spy obeys.

"So! You are a cur, dreaming with your eyes open! You are not *all* humility, it seems. How do you feel about the king, now that he has brought you to this? Grateful? Bitter? Compose yourself."

"The king is the king. Nothing can change that."

"Can it not?"

"My feelings are smoke; no one can catch them."

"Why did he do this?"

"I cannot say, majesty."

"Spare me titles. You are the slave in the parade, whose eyes call me other things. Do you think I cannot hear that stiff shout that bobs and cannot bow between your legs? You own a dwarf taller than its master. He did it because he does not believe in himself."

"When was happiness easy to believe? Imagine Cassandra with a smile!"

"I had no Greek to make me glib, a woman. The king could not believe in his luck. I am not enough for him, my love. Why? *Why?* You know as well as I do, but you will not say. Is that loyalty in you, coward silence? You despise in others what you lack the nerve to see in yourself: your pride has no sun. You love yourself in the dark and think it manhood. I will tell you what you know: he does not love himself enough. Happiness leaves him short. That is the cheap door which let you in. You are what he truly loves; not for your looks or your caresses – am I simple there, or not? – but for your qualities: he fears you finer, stronger, better than himself."

"Not any more."

"Now you interrupt, when I am being beautiful. What we were we always are, except happy."

"Happiness is not in nature; man is incomplete and alone tries to furnish it."

"You are all quotations."

"From unwritten works."

"Because I smile does not mean that I like you. I dislike you. You are what he thought he should be, when he should have been himself. Well?"

"I hope your majesty is wrong."

"He believes in your desire when he cannot believe in his own. The thoroughbred consults the cur. He would put you on like a coat. Lydia is not enough for him, because he is not enough for Lydia, though she thought him so. Your envy matters more to him than Lydia's love. I thought him a man; I see I was wrong. You are the proof. He is a coward and a fool and I loved him. What am I?"

"Lydia."

"You begin to be hopeful, whatever your name is. Don't tell me. Your face belongs to a courtier; one head droops, the other not. One of you is lying; only the human can."

The queen does not cover herself. Gyges can imagine the king, on his way to Lydia's bed.

"He wanted me to know how happy he was. Nothing more. He wanted a witness. Can you not understand that?"

"You tell the truth as if it were a lie; and I believe it. You are the witness; he is the crime. I understand perfectly, don't I?"

"Is it not flattering?"

"Question and answer stuff! Do I need flattery? Look at me!"

"I see what you mean."

A pause makes common patients of the queen and her subject. "Your report," Lydia says, "what will it say? Great tits? Brilliant bum? Are you smiling? Do you dare?"

"Majesty ... my commitment was to see, not to speak. He wants only to know that I know what he knows."

"Although you never can! Can dust know the gods?"

"Dangerous ground! Might we move a little lower?"

"Do not think to protect yourself by protecting me. There was sure to be a report. He wants to see you, does he not?"

"No arrangement has been made."

"Where? Where have the things which have not been arranged been arranged? You follow me perfectly well. I want to see you both. I want to be your witness, who shall also be your judge. Arrange it. There is no alternative."

"Your majesty flatters me. I hope ..."

"That lame luxury I shall deny you. Abandon hope; you are already here."

"My knowledge was all he required, of what he and no other man enjoyed. My eyes and not my tongue were to be his pleasure."

"He *and* no other man! That sounds like two distinct people. Your friend has given me a lover."

"That, I am sure, is the last thing he wants."

"And the last he shall have."

She was there and she was gone. He was alone and in her company. He wore the invisible shackle of her wishes. She had watched him put himself together, the clothes, and he hardly had the strength to be their hanger. She went and seemed to take him with her. He was superfluous to himself, an irritation. He was her thing, the devil.

She wore her usual, priceless shift as she came from the door of her dressing room to where the king was waiting. Her fall broke nothing; there was no telling bruise. What was different? Nothing; nothing was different, but who could tell? The king waited in primed ignorance, thick with his secret. Who whom, said the oracle.

Gyges trembled, refusing office after election to it. He could have been dead; he was alive. He stole into himself, a thief stowed in a sleeve of flesh. What lay ahead? A future! Can the wheel stop because of what the dust declares? He was mounted on an axle which rolled without his volition. He slunk swaggering through the golden palace, rimmed with the king's ring, privileged nullity, authorised to be vain.

The man who has tasted poison imagines that he is proof against its mortal threat. He feels better for his escape, although the stuff has declared its war. Do not all battles begin with birdsong? Gyges has got off lightly, he thinks. He thinks and thinks and lightness floats him above the city, fatuous immortal. He tastes the queen's words on his own tongue; he savours them again. Their mettle is sweet; their bite sharpens his own. He walks on arcaded air, the heat of the city tricked with unsharable shadows: he is cool where others burn. Other women smile at him (some verify their breasts) and the actor believes that they would do as well. Gyges recognises the statistician in himself; it is the libertine's only liberty, to count.

Lydia was in her husband's bed. Gyges' gaze curried her body. The king tasted his unknown friend and believed him the woman. He was never so passionate; she never so desirable, or desiring. She piped encouragement like a boy inspiring infantry! He was sure that he had done something right. What he forced upon her she could not resist; pleasure slapped her left and right – oh the thickness of her slim throat, with the blood working in it! – and her eyes glared for the charge. Treachery is an expert hedonist, the double agent.

She denied nothing. She agreed to be amazed. She threw shame aside, the cluttering garment. Fake and fancy salted common sweat. She had made him king; she could unmake him too. What pleasure – in the meanwhile – to be subject to his business! He came to her as to an office and thought himself at home, the king. He did to her what she was doing to him and thought it proved his wit and power. The fool never heard his bells. The woman's yes, yes, yes confirmed his folly. The cock can crow at affirmations too.

Soft coins of speech passed between them, warm from the close pockets of their mouths. Small change can warp the world; a whisper of grass splits the flag. How does the greening nail sap through stone? What threads its blade between the granite's wink?

They had, till then, been each other's secret, king and queen, hermetic pair. Nothing could come between them, not even the day. Love was their untimely treasure, unguessed gold secreted in a golden place, escaping public inventory. Couched in their official bed, they trumped Midas and touched each other to life. They cheapened gold. Together they had – *had*! – subverted monarchy by making something common that was the lord of sovereignty. King and queen were crowned with each other. Now what was left of that airless complicity in which nothing (she swore) could come between them? Now she was enlightened. Her eyes were open while his were shut. She saw it all.

The night chamberlain smirked beyond the studded doors. His ears glimpsed new things through the cedar. His sketchy mind fleshed ingenuities. He supplemented mutters and sharps like a sordid scholar. His mind's eye was a scrutinising tool. He did his duty. The guard who keeps a secret is its incorruptible betrayer: trust him. The straight face always knows the joke, or that there is one. And there always is.

The king laughed, but he did not know the joke. The queen and he had a secret from each other: Gyges. True! But the king had no notion that their secrets were the same. That was the difference. The queen, betrayed, was richer than her traitor. She possessed the king's secret, who had only his own.

In those hours, however many days or nights figured in their calendar, Lydia was a new country. She was valleyed and peaked with tangible originality. The king was her explorer; he set new fire to new nerve. Had they been happy before, he and she, in their darkness? They were – he would swear – happier now. He and Lydia worked at their gaping pleasure like miners in a hot, black place, buried in each other.

Parody is more shameless than the real thing. Shadows outweigh substance. Is that the hell of it?

Gyges' life was as full as an egg. Not for a moment did he wonder what to do. He wondered only what would happen. Imagination was the yolk that fed him and composed him. He saw her everywhere. His vacant hours were clocked with waiting, though none could see (or be told of) his attendance. Indenture made him reckless in speech and address. He snarled in his unbarred cage and prowled to admiration like a beast sloping sullenly to his keeper's dish. Steeped in negation, he counted back from the moment of her dreaded summons. He craved fear and she was teaching him, with her savage remand, not to fear it.

Reckless in speech and address, he visited his relatives and mocked their fat resignation; they were sumptuously content in their fidelity to the king. When they said how surprised they were by Candaules' qualities, he congratulated them on their blind astuteness. His family promoted him with their suspicions. Had he always seemed so exhilarated? Had he always been so handsome? His mother thought he looked particularly well (and urged him to take care). His swagger made a snob of her: she talked about their lineage. He sighed affably at her antique prattle, and was primed by it: a princely past was planted ahead of him. Lies offered more freedom than truth; that commodity could be racked from any slave.

He rode through Lydia like a conqueror who uses a truce for reconnaissance. Alone, he rehearsed a parade. When he reached the city, the walls of the palace no longer noticed him. He could step through them at will. Ramparts of dust, he swam through them like the sun. The machinery of the state was a toy he could squat to play with. Expert, he turned it over and quizzed its unalarmed anatomy. The world sloughed its intimidating scale; his naughty hand put on its pattern like a glove. He could amble through the eye of a needle without pinching his ambition. His mistake? He did not dream; he was dreamed.

How long did she play him? How long is a parenthesis? How much can a fence enclose? Why do men go into dangerous places and first score their limits? Is vacancy made valuable by the promise of walls? Desolation becomes a prize if someone claims title to it. Gyges' mind was turreted with the logic of his state. His folly made him

wise. He waited and he waited. Cursed by freedom's lease, he fretted for captivity. He had plans.

Two men came one day in a commissioned style. A slave was scraping oil from his exercised shoulders. He was brackish with dust from his gallop. The slave thumbed soft crust from the strigil. Gyges invited another cull with an indicative finger by his shoulder blade. His eyes cued the men. Which one was to say it? "Lord Gyges..."

"I shan't be a second."

They took him to the armoury in the palace. This time, he imagined neither death nor preferment. He was merely curious. There were spears and swords, daggers and axes, serried for privileged selection. The blades were brilliant, and edgy for blood.

The king was going bald. Sweat haloed his crown. He looked like a god, the better for age. Young gods have problems with authority; the old wield it. The females are different and – in their absence – to be smiled at: they make the boys of us.

"Well, my friend?"

"Your majesty is in health? It follows that the rest of us are so."

"You haven't changed. How long has it been?"

"Between commands I mark no punctuation, sire."

"Gyges the incorrigible! It's been too long."

"Stands corrected, sire."

The king rummages in his throat for a new voice, and finds one. "You saw her." He looks at weapons. "What did you think?"

"I received no commission to think."

"I commission you now."

"Your majesty did not exaggerate. She is everything you said; and did not."

"That is everything indeed! You concede that I must be the happiest man in the world?"

"You have that obligation; how should I not own it?"

"Choose a weapon. We can exercise. The queen proposed we should. She has ... I was going to say 'changed', but no: she has become even more herself. More passionate about me than ever. And also more concerned. Gyges?"

"Still here."

"She suggested this. That I should ask my dearest, most trusted friend to come and train with me. These banquets undo a man's belt. You see? There's nothing she doesn't think of for me!"

"So I see."

"I'm relying on you, Gyges, so is she. Sabre? Rapier? Quarter-staff? Gyges, I'm so happy to see you. Embrace me first and then we'll fight."

In the gallery, where sergeants clocked the guards at drill, Lydia watched. Her husband and the other man leaned chest to chest. Their frowns were smiles avoiding the obvious; she caught the rustle of their whispers. The small change of laughter passed between them as they traded in her beauty (so she read them) in a currency that made them one, and two. The queen's vanity fattened on their conspiracy. She had been beautiful; she became a beauty, the created thing. She had loved; now she wanted. The flower at its peak has peaked.

"Why not swords?"

She had come through a small door, up a screw of steps

whose walls were garrulous with soldiers' scribbles, last-
ing ephemera. She was barracked by their obscenity. The
air she now breathed came from the heat beneath her. It
had a flavour as it passed her nostrils. Buoyed among the
motes, her flesh glossed her with sensation, but it made no
choice: she was in suspense between the two men. She
could believe, for a wishful moment, that she envied them:
each was decidedly who he was; she, alone, lacked decision. Her weapon was chosen, but she did not hold it, or
know who did. Now she was blank, in attendance on the
men.

"Defend yourself, my friend. I warn you: I'm stronger
now. I hope that you are. Do me no favours; that's an
order, *and* advice. It might be dangerous."

Choice; comparison; agreement; places. She watched
their tasselled commerce in loneliness. Chalked soles
squeaked and patterned the alternating floor. Feet bruised
the stone. Arms rose and fell; blades skirled in rough
music. Sunlight ran over their bodies like spilled heat. Silk
shadows tried leggings on them and unhosed them again,
eclipsed and released them into sun-gashed scowls. Hot
helmets metalled their heads with light and left them
gleaming (the king's especially). The marble warmed to
them.

Lydia breathed dust in the grained gallery. Its high air
put a choker to her throat. Her nostrils waxed to find suf-
ficient breath. Superfluousness exercised her.

In her light and in ignorance of her, they rehearsed
death on the armoury floor. Ready to die for each other,
playful enemies, they were both up for Lydia. They would
have gone together at once to kill strangers, who now

feinted and lunged their promises to each other, mindless of her compromising eyes. Their swords met and met. Old friends, they were each other on the noisy floor. Responding to response, each man meeting himself in his opponent, sweet, sweating continuity, we two fought; you two fought. How would it end?

"Tired, Gyges? Should we two stop?"

"If his majesty is tired, his majesty must say."

"Defend yourself, my friend. A king is never tired."

For how long did the queen stand in the gallery under the shipwrights' ceiling, watching the men play at enmity? What was she thinking, Lydia? *Was* she thinking? Did she fancy she could have them both? Had she been more vicious, she might have been more generous. Had she been literate, she might have known the part. But Lydia knew no books, except accountants' clay. Her love was love; it had no precedent. When she thought herself loved, she took it for the first time. The thing sprang words as clean as leaves veined with her true blood. She and the king had been what she and he could not hope to be again. Innocence may meet pain; it can never expect it.

Untrained in the grammar of suspicion (common caution has no royal ring), the queen had had no lessons in the future tense. Words came unused to her; she might have minted them. She spoke in clear notes. She assumed them music. Mindless of will or might – for her yesterday was seamless with today – flux and changelessness posed no antithesis to the Lydia that was.

High-born, she was cousin to the gods who found seats set for them on the crest of Sipylos. What immortal, borrowing ease, ever wondered whose servility plumped accommodation a deity could take for granted? It is alien to the fearless to wonder why things have been done, or where they might be leading. Gods have this weakness: they cannot foresee the craven or imagine the base. They cannot be outwitted, but they can be fooled.

"We can always stop."

There is no conventional wisdom in the queen; education has not taught her folly. She lives in the present, a pupil with no other branch of language on which to swing. She constructs everything from the tense she knows. The men skip, turn, clash, smile on the fretful floor. Is she still there, the queen? How long has this been going on? She cannot say; she does not deal in calibrated accuracies. The court is a place of orders and wishes, not of diaries or metric calculation. Lydia spells in blood, not letters; her words come candied with colour.

She has no humour, is that the truth? Humour confesses humanity, the common touch. Comedy and errors are down the hall from each other; they share a low title. Queens are amused (or not); they cannot be expected to amuse. For the courtier, laughter may be a duty, but it cannot be volunteered. Queens are humoured; they admit faults only to measure the promptness of their denial. Who agrees with a monarch's self-criticism is that monarch's trusted enemy. Acquiescence turns keys, and coats.

Did the queen lack wit? She had no aptitude for paradox. She never generalised. Her integrity was also her lameness: she could put forward only one foot at a time. She hoped for nothing from either of them (hope was born in a box, like a slave); she had expectations, which were her own.

The two are suited in sweat. The woman is dry. Their feet blue the marble. The king had turned Lydia into his friend's whore. Should she love him? The friend had enjoyed her with his eyes. Should she hate him? Could she forgive a king who paraded her in the same precinct where a knobbed dwarf could smirk his choice, where women were one meat? Or the friend, could he be pardoned, who consented to be ignoble out of fear or tact (its diplomatic face)? Perhaps disdain (fear's rogue brother) ushered Gyges into the *camera obscura* which jacked her world upside down as a man makes a wheelbarrow of a drab. As she turned possibilities on the wheel of her mind, they whirled into patterned elegance, despite herself. They began almost to amuse her. Bastard, cripple, underling, who should match their calculated patience, their inventive malice, their servile arrogance? She had known a man; she began to know men. Those who first despise themselves are schooled, if they endure, into shamelessness; contempt breeds familiarity.

When did her expression change? When did she feel the temptation to call "time", as one might a servant? Her pendulum began, at some point, to swing. Her condescension switched to something less gracious, which could not fall equally on both of those who, all unconsciously, worked below her. How dare they take independent pleasure in each other? Complacent in their exercise, this dud duel revived their parity. Its complicity dethroned her.

Their panting conversation – turn and turn about on the creased flags – was feathered with ground-floor whispers, lacking the lift to come to her. Those wingless words followed the tideline of their own ebb and flow on the unmortared floor; their dainty wilfulness made Lydia a futile moon. They whispered her into irrelevance, the queen! The two of them made a republic of her monarchy, who was their mistress. Which should she blame? How could she be sure when their common air came up to choke her?

"Tired, your majesty?"

"As a lion, Gyges. I slipped is all."

"Do lions slip, sir?"

Will they go on forever? Something slithers between them like a flat snake. They flinch from the serpent shadow, look up, the two of them, for its source. The queen's arm provides their forked intruder.

Discovering herself, she has advanced to the gallery's rail. She leans into the sun and falls at their feet a disembodied scarf, even as she stands high above them in her majesty. The men look at her and – as if no disinclination were involved – at each other, once more. They smile indeed. The queen too is smiling. Are they all then doing the same thing at the same time?

This is nice. They laugh at how nice it is. What joke merits that triple sound? Each of the men, in furtive industry, could supply an unrepeatable jest, and that is what amuses them perhaps. Can Lydia possibly know the one they know? No mercenary sergeant has debauched her ear. She has not been recruited, as males are, and stripped of soft illusions. Shaved boys must jettison unbearded tenderness on the common tip; girls can keep their curls and are unobliged to vile unison. Female dreams know no foul-mouthed parade. Divorce precedes marriage here. The first casualty of war is love's anatomy. The deputed corporal hoists all mothers' skirts with his split fingers. He dares the booted babies to break ranks in their defence. Mum, they smirk maturity at his command. Mother becomes another stale. Who would go home to her?

Neither man can look at the queen and not know what she does not know, and not be known to know. Similarities distinguish them.

"Don't stop for me."

"Have we stopped? You have stopped us. And why not? Let us stop, my friend. We can have something to drink. You must be tired." Command and solicitude tread in each other's tracks. Should Gyges be tired for the king's sake? He bows. One hand rests on his knee before, with a flick of the neck, his eyes go up in insolent obeisance. "This," the king calls, as if she were further away, so that courtesy flirts with rebuff, "is the friend of whom I spoke. The one you wanted . . ."

"I know."

"Gyges, my friend . . . the queen."

He has looked up too soon and can correct insolence only by compounding it. He does not blink. "Your majesty's most humble servant." He raises himself the better to bend again, the actor.

"Have we not met before?" Who – the queen's mildness puts the question – will now accuse me of wanting humour? "Pray continue with your exercise. I mustn't disturb you when you are doing each other so much good."

"We can stop whenever you like." The king's tone unlimbers him. Oh for that bath! "Just say."

"Have you had enough, the pair of you? Are you no longer up to it?"

How natural men are when they are false! The king gives Gyges such an easy look, embracing the queen and humanising her; his face is all inquiry: well? "If her majesty wishes it," the prompt courtier replies, "I am up to anything."

Reluctance, playing eager, might have schemed for the encore. It dresses the battle more realistic than it was before. Audiences promise criticism; royal preferment. They must do better, the men, than in rehearsal, or they will curse themselves.

Sword sharpens sword; they scrap and scrape. There and there and there, the men move. They collide, break and recur. Tiredness makes for sincerity; it abbreviates style. Their patter teases the queen. How was that? Arrangement or accident? Better? Worse? They work; they play.

Lydia appreciates their reprise. She almost sees them one. Does she love them equally now or does she hate them equally? How should she separate love and hate any better than one man from another? Duel and duet, can they be two?

The see-saw soars and pitches in the same motion. Who will cry "cut" and make conferring critics of them all?

At the pivotal point, she neither falls nor rises with their oscillation. Privy to their antagonism, she is not part of it.

They fight to a standstill, bereft of a climax. They look to her.

"You're as good as each other! Nothing to choose between you! Can you possibly be trying? Or are you both on the same side?"

"We're old friends."

"Old, are you?"

"And trying to remain so." The king speaks for both of them, as both could never speak. "Friends."

Lydia shows her elbows on the parapet; winged, her heels leave the narrow floor. She plays a girlish corporal. "Will you do me a favour?"

"I will do anything you ask," her husband replies, "but it can never be a favour."

Feet down, she lets her jaw go sideways, a good mark implied. "And you?" She throws the question like a bone.

"What the king has said, I should like to say. More than anything."

Both men are decidedly neat. "I thank you both," she says. Her throat is supple now and pure of dust. "Kill him," she says.

They hear. Hearing is an act. It takes time. She wants one of them dead, they hear, they hear, but which? Subject and object construe no distinction. They wait for a prompt, actors who have taken the cue but are corpsed for the response. She observes their freeze and melts it, with unrepetition: "Kill him." There is neither anger nor malice in her tone, rather a certain encouragement, as one might say, "Yes, yes," to those who cannot believe their luck before a treat.

Would they find male purpose in a woman's tone? She

can invite; she cannot perform. She is the sheath; they have the swords. The queen's command is the queen's pleasure; she has no mind to wait much longer. "Kill him, I said."

"Who's whom?"

The queen is urgent; it coarsens her perhaps (a male view?). Unschooled in playful postponement, she has no tooth for succulent secrecy. She cannot imagine how the three of them might contrive an elastic triangle and laugh at the unbending world.

What is more complicated than ABC?

Pretence can make reality a clown, but Lydia will not have it. The triangle is not her form; three and two will not make one with her. Geometry belongs to slaves. She will be no party to equilateral ease. Are there any really good games for three?

Lydia would know what happens next, and now. She is in no mood for meditative strolls. She has thought enough and been thought too much. Consideration bores her; she wants the future, and immediately. The men have had their fun; she will brook no more rehearsal. "Kill him."

Is the fight less enthusiastic now? Reality is slow on cue and clumsily presented. There is never enough time for its perfection. The two make weary patterns on the used marble. Their weapons are sharper than they are. Counterfeit amusement jumps between them, like a tired child who ought to be in bed. Its false liveliness bills them for spontaneities they cannot meet. As if complicity remained unflawed, they wince where recently they smiled. What is fair play when cheat is the game?

In the breathing clinch, jammed hilt to hilt, the king pants for time out. "What does she mean?"

"What she says, doesn't she?" Gyges wants a scholar's gloss. "What else can she?"

"What do we do?" Candaules has no scholarship (the Greek reported him so). He is now a bald boy, and commoner. "She can tell we're not fighting seriously."

Gyges bends metal on metal; arms are roped with effort. The two men strain and stay in tandem. "What do you suggest?" Deference touches on presumption. The king is dry of invention. Gyges presses: "Think of something!"

"She's playing with us," the king dares to hope. "We'll play with her! Hit hard. Fear not. Be realistic. Play for time."

"Kill him." The voice claps them to business. Bending to, they rig a clever fight; they excel themselves. The old ground is renewed: they leap onto the dais; they vault; they find spring in the trampoline. Where black bolsters hang on ropes for boxers they lunge and dodge and agree on tricks. A bellied bag dangles like a legless eunuch on the gallows. A windy slash from one man unzips its tripes; another dumps it on the floor. Grinning, the two strive to dupe the queen with furious fraud.

Masked by the stiff horse recruits must fork, Candaules' words pass like contraband: "Can she suspect?" Gyges cannot help him. "Can she know?"

"How can I say?"

"Look at her."

Their simultaneous tribute vexes the queen. "Kill him," she calls down. "He knows."

The men are done with clash and clatter. They want that bath, that drink. They could use a laugh. How did this start? They scamper, crouch, falter, slip. Exhaustion lends them angry energy. Damn choreography, they want an end to this. They raise heavy arms and fall against each other; neither knows who is supporting the other or whose will be the star. Their swords are toothy; edges gone.

In gasping absurdity, blades collide, collude. Gyges strikes with both arms. Unless he has won, he has lost; his breast exposed, his blade locked to the floor. The king's sword is a sudden icicle; it melts in his hand, snapped to water. Candaules holds its hilt like an unpaired mitten. His other hand is beautiful, the long fingers. "All right, my friend," he says, "enough!"

Disarmed, the king is silvered in spent reserve. His confidence in Gyges invites a draw, but cannot deserve it. Gyges makes a rumpled face. He looks at the king for the first time as one who need not be courtly, but who will. In brazen choice, Gyges is entirely himself. What should he do but laugh, for the moment? For the moment, he does; the king too. Should we two take this woman seriously? Can she divide us?

The men are not smiling as they reconsider. The king looks up at Lydia, reliant on what he just discounted. Gyges too looks up. The men's unvisored amity, they seem to say, has overruled the queen. The king blows her a kiss. He winks at Gyges, the sweat!

A bee buzzes in the settling air of the armoury. It means something to Gyges; it may mean something to the queen. To the king, it means nothing.

"What are you smiling at?"

"Nothing."

Gyges sees them a pair for the last time. He shortens his blade and thrusts it – both hands! – into the king's liver. The point of the weapon makes a nipple in the royal belly. The king dumps on one knee before his friend. A brief bow and he goes to the floor. His bleeding case decreases at Gyges' clenched feet. He is up; he is down.

"Is this what you really want?"

When Gyges looks up, the queen has gone. Was she ever there? Her voice leaves a message. "Wait there."

Gyges is alone, and pointless. His sword wilts. What is success without another? He hears her footfall. In a flutter of light, fluked with attendant shadows, Lydia pedals down the twist of stairway from the catwalk to the armoury floor. Gyges is now alone. He has succeeded.

"I presume you *were* speaking to me."

"I am the queen. Remember that."

"And I am going to be the king."

"The king is the man whom the queen elects to marry."

Gyges looks at his sword, dipstick oiled with the king's guts. "I am the man who plays the king by taking the queen. You want a man of whom there is nothing you cannot imagine. I am that man, and you know it."

"Your insolence is beyond belief."

"Depend upon it."

How should Lydia distinguish contempt from respect, desire from disgust, remorse from opportunity? She cannot; it modernises her.

"We have arrangements to make."

Gyges is hairier; his loins are thick. His stance is alien; the woman is booty. She waits on him.

"They all think you're the same queen. Tell them that he tried to kill you. He was not a man; you were the unseeded evidence he wanted to suppress. He had to be rid of you, if he wanted to keep the throne. He was a traitor who wanted to take Lydia for his own family; that way we can be done with all of them."

Gyges indicates the hanging gang of bags. The one with a drool of tripes to the floor conveys the lesson. Lydia's eyes evade the evidence. They would flit with the flower-less bee: where is it exactly? "I don't know that I can," she says.

"You can; you will. Cook up something with tears in its recipe."

"How could he? How could you?"

"Words which will undoubtedly furnish the repertoire. Play the woman, Lydia; be the queen. Leave the rest to me."

"How long has this been in your mind?"

"A long time. Half an hour. I never knew till then, when his voice went grey with tiredness, that I was truly his master, and had always been. I *imagined*, but any slave can have ideas! I hoped; I feared; I could never know. Until now. Now I am certain. What was his is mine; including you."

"He was mine. I was not his. I shall call the guard and tell them the truth."

"Do you know it? If you do, they lack the wit to follow it. Tell them lies – they can be swallowed without water."

"You and he are both traitors."

"He and I are no longer both. He is dead; I am what you want, the only man alive who possibly can be."

"Take me in the king's blood. Can you?"

Gyges can; Gyges does.

The thread of his spit in her beard, she looks at herself and quickens to womanhood. She might be snatching an angry dress from her cupboard. "You'll never be to me what he was."

"Never. I promise."

She wipes his stuff with the edge of her robe. "I can never love – or even hate – you."

"Your feelings can go in your drawer. You desire me and I desire you. That will do. Our reasons differ, but we shall always be together; conspiracy outlasts feelings. Politics are only muddied by sincerity; we'll none of it. His blood is our bond; his brush will stain us both."

"Don't touch me."

"I shall do as I please, and as you please, whether you please or not. What you want and what you say you want will never square; you will never have the two at the same time. You loved him; you'll want me. I shall touch you as and when I like. Put your hand in his mess. There. And I'll do the same. Soft and wet, like a woman. Like it? Now take my hand. Take my hand."

The fingers marry in the king's sauce. She gasps and gasps again. Pain and pleasure jam each other's lines. Hate reassures her; can it still be hate?

"We must stick together. I will not let you go until his mortar dries on us. You were right to despise him, Lydia; look what he has brought you to. *Look*." Her wet hem, heavy with his shot, touches them both. "You were not enough for him, who would have been too much for anyone else. What have you lost? What have you gained?

Nothing; everything. Everything? Nothing!"

"He loved me."

"That was his weakness. Your cruelty was to make him happy. Disappointment he might have taken like a man; in paradise, he could only be a weed. Your treachery lay in exceeding his hopes. You cannot exceed mine; hence your fidelity, and my confidence."

"I am not in your class. Don't instruct me. Your reasoning bores me: spare me your Greek. Take me without apology, because you're right: then at least we can abandon sincerity for the bore it is."

"On your knees, woman, for a start. Be clever for me; I think you can. Is that what you want? Isn't it? You want what you don't want, and you shall have it. Doubt me; I can be sure of that. It destroyed him; it strengthens me."

"Don't talk: be my dog, paw my breasts."

He left them to nurse the floor. Her command was his pleasure, its refusal. "Don't do that" lent him ambition, who did not need it. She smiled her rage. The larder of their future was shelved with tasty tricks. Had she not learned that men can pump blood and think of tax returns? Silences too can contradict. Command the brutal, you license the sly. What tyrant fails to recruit a clever secretariat? You follow?

Gyges made a throne of the queen.

Slaves came and took care of the housekeeping. The under-privileged are used to corpses. Courtiers considered the queen. Ambition stops at no crime; they saw nothing amiss.

"This," she said, " is the king." Her words crowned Gyges. "Close *his* eyes; they've seen enough."

Gyges, elected by her single vote, was cast. Living by the old clock, the courtiers took their time from Lydia. The adjustment did not change their hours; they could not see the crack, who only heard the whip.

Lydia's choice was her country's obligation. She announced the dead man's execution. His family was disgraced (there is always a wicked uncle, who explains it all). Gyges' people came to town. He was Lydia's champion; she was lucky to have him. He seemed to fill a smaller part than that of king; the queen, diminished, appeared greater than before. She was more visible. Her wardrobe was soon too full to admit the slimmest addition.

Candaules became proverbial. Schoolchildren chanted him an ass. His death was denied its tragedy; farce stuffed the memory of him with laughs. He was the clown who had paid for a painting by giving the artist – an Egyptian, wasn't he? – its weight in gold. He had wanted to please the queen; and had, by making himself ridiculous. Candaules was a common name in Lydia and now its owners played the fool.

Gyges changed all the locks. What wise thief does not? First, he went to the barracks. The men drilled and polished. In the yard, chariots bowed on unhorsed traces,

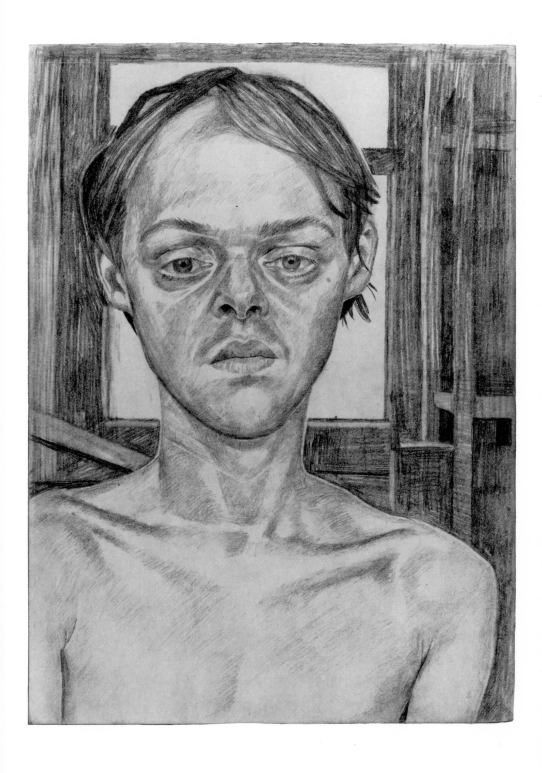

while their wheels were righted. Everyone was busy;
Gyges would find no volunteers.

He took two heavy javelins from the common rack.
The first he flung into the eye of the hooped target. Then,
as it hung quivering, he split it, toe to tip, with the second,
whose prick shared the bull. Any questions? He had
spoken well. The men were his. Their graffiti chalked
him king.

Gyges became a man of morality. Carefree youth made
him think of war, their curb. The Greek cities looked to
their gates. He had the key: gold went to the oracles and
made amenable locksmiths of them.

He never bought art; no one could call him Candaules.
He deplored loud laughter, but his predecessor sometimes
tickled him. He was keen on justice, the king's. He sat on
the bench in dull cases and enlivened them with courteous
attentions. He appreciated a lawyer who could make
something authorise what it was never intended to sanc-
tion. He felt the force of argument like something
palpable.

Plaintiffs complained of his fairness more often than
defendants. He gave women chairs; old men were
refreshed. He passed sentence like water, with a grave
sigh.

His justice could be pedantic, his orders capriciously
precise. An heir accused his brother of denying him access
to a distant farm. Gyges decreed that the plaintiff be
admitted to the premises at once. In triumph, the brother
hurried to take possession. Once in the bricked heat, he
lost his appetite for rural life. He found grinning soldiers
at the tight door. Gyges had ordered him admitted; he

refused him exit. The soldiers threw him the name Candaules, like a meatless bone, the dog. The sporting loser stayed at court and went hunting with his king.

Gyges rode home to unhorsed accountants, businessmen. He always wanted to know where he stood. The man in the distant farm was his unknowing cousin: Gyges too became an indoors man. He was not disposed to exercise in the armoury; he never invited old friends. Those two flung spears were his warrant; they badged his legend, which knew no encore, nor needed one.

Gyges never sought popularity. To be largely liked is to have enemies. He chose to be enigmatic. Puzzles raise doubts in those who cannot solve them: they always think there must be something wrong with them, never the puzzle. Frowns keep people busy.

The king is determined to make Lydia safe, for himself, for her. Is this one ambition or two? He wants Lydia for himself: does the queen come into that? And how? The two of them, he and Lydia, Lydia and he, are triune in their duplicity. She sees two of him (the man, the king) and he thinks himself but one. He sees two of her (head and tail).

Solus Rex.

Alone, he was obliged to be with her. When he saw another, it was in her light. If he went away, he found himself lessened; being himself was not an improvement. He longed for routines which, when he had to live them, excited fugitive thoughts. Warm and together, the fire at their feet, wine cheating on the hearth, clever guests due, they had everything they could ask for, nothing more.

Desire doubled with disdain. It made Lydia sleek; he

was stiff at the sight of her. (Boredom and bedroom make an economic anagram.) Formality cooled their bed, its puncture lent it heat. "Do that," she said, denied. ("Don't" he always did.)

Their court was a place of drills and precedents. They advertised for the best, and only the best did not apply. Uniforms embroidered; speech grew fatuous brocade: nothing but courteous ceremony. Gyges had at all times to be recognised as king. It was an honour to attend him at stool. His behind was a place of advancement.

His steady undisclosed dread was that one day, looking in the yellow mirror of the palace, he might see his old friend leaping to retrieve his place. He feared he might be jumped. He went about in slippers, to be wise to footsteps at his back.

He wanted to be more than a sceptred king. He craved ubiquity; he would be all over Lydia, all of the time. He looked at the ring which Candaules had given him, the mirror of his treachery. His friend looked at him from his ideogram. He thought of the brother in the bricked farm. He sent men to be sure he was dead, and buried. The king looked at him still.

He went to the armoury and earned the smith's respect with admiration. He took a rasp from the bench and, while the bellows panted metal red, he effaced his friend.

The scored blank offended him. He rubbed and rubbed until the scores were even. The blank winked like an accomplice. What mark might flag the kingdom as his? He rubbed and rubbed until his own image posed in the blank. He sent for an Ephesian and his linen roll of tools.

Lydia said, "It's very like you."

He clenched his metalled fist and punched it on the face of Lydia. His engraved ring, that is to say, stamped the first coin out of gold which never ceased to accumulate in the royal treasury. He stamped and stamped again, minting ubiquity. The coins bore his face to every corner of the kingdom. Unalloyed, his authority bounded across Lydia, and her boundaries: he acquired a seashore and poets other than the one he wanted, Archilochos whose pleasure (from a distance) was not to please. He died, the recusant, as hired muscle, on some insular mission. His grave, the poet's, buzzed with stings, the Muse's obituary. Who cared?

The pregnant queen approved her husband's policy. The future and the past wrapped the present in her womb. She knew the tenses now all right. Her belly would be striped with them.

Gyges welcomed the boy. It bore his stamp. He taught the prince to run and jump and how to throw a spear. He tolerated his misses. He loved and hated the young man, whom Lydia loved and loved. The prince was undoubtedly hers; he had come from the sheath of her womb like a soft sword drawn from her bloody scabbard. Was he as certainly Gyges'? Was the boy his, or *his*? The oracle, chrysostomised, promised him the real thing.

When the prince threw the spear, he threw it, one day, as well as his father, whoever his father was. When he jumped, he landed in his father's traces. Had he tried as hard as he could? He swore he had. Did that make him a rival or a diplomat? Was he coming or had he arrived?

Lydia and Gyges lived long years in the richest kingdom in Anatolia. Gyges grew fatter and fatter. He watched his weight and foreign doctors were hired to be blamed for it. He took exercise which left him regularly out of breath. He was a generous host who counted his wealth on the abacus of his guests' widening eyes. His gifts made slaves of them. He ceased to go abroad in person; his money toured for him. His donations established pillared temples and banked favours in a dozen sites. Oracles lost their teeth on his sweets.

Ambassadors reported singular harmony at Sardis. There was, they were sorry to say, no way of using the one against the other, such was the royal proximity. They were like close-set stones that need no mortar and cannot be filed apart.

Lydia's beauty had a long, long summer and an exquisite autumn. Gyges' hair went from his head to his chest, it seemed; he wore a virile shirt. When he and his queen retired (to bed, to bed), courtiers feared their wives might be disappointed that they lacked the king's address. No scandal soured the air of the capital. Lydia and the king seemed to take undying pleasure in each other.

The palace walls were whitened with marble, exclusive show. The shutters were armed with reinforcing bars.

The nightly guard was sometimes teased by the king; he concealed a friend, now and again, in a secret niche to test the sentries' diligence. He was entertained when they jumped him (the friend).

Lydia was a byword for cleanliness. The king and queen abominated dirt. They wanted only to be themselves. Each night the Captain of the Guard reported, through the chased door, "No strangers, majesties."

The royal pair alone could see Candaules. He was the wide-eyed, invisible man no pennies could blind, no grave enclose. In his unblinking sight their every action was performed. His vigilance could never be escaped.